Charles Follen Adams, Morgan J. Sweeney

Leedle Yawcob Strauss

And Other Poems

Charles Follen Adams, Morgan J. Sweeney

Leedle Yawcob Strauss
And Other Poems

ISBN/EAN: 9783743382527

Manufactured in Europe, USA, Canada, Australia, Japa

Cover: Foto ©Andreas Hilbeck / pixelio.de

Manufactured and distributed by brebook publishing software (www.brebook.com)

Charles Follen Adams, Morgan J. Sweeney

Leedle Yawcob Strauss

Leedle Yawcob Strauss,

AND OTHER POEMS.

By CHARLES F. ADAMS.

With Sixty-five Illustrations
By "BOZ."

BOSTON:
LEE AND SHEPARD, PUBLISHERS.
NEW YORK:
CHARLES T. DILLINGHAM.
1878.

ELECTROTYPED BY
O. J. PETERS & SON,
73 FEDERAL STREET,
BOSTON.

PREFACE.

———◆———

It is with some misgivings that the author, at the solicitation of many, perhaps over-zealous friends, has ventured to place this little volume before the public. The writer, moving only in the mercantile world, feels that he has wandered into forbidden ground, and craves the indulgence of the *literati* for these attempts to "woo the Muse" during the few leisure hours allowed to members of his vocation.

With the invaluable co-operation of "Boz" (Mr. M. J. Sweeney), — whose happy delineations form a prominent feature of attraction, — the author expresses the hope that this volume may meet with the kindly reception that has been accorded to many of the individual selections which have appeared from time to time in our local papers, "Scribner's Monthly," "Detroit Free Press," and other publications.

PREFACE.

That its crudities may be excused by reason of the writer's non-familiarity with matters so foreign to his daily routine of business life, and that "Leedle Yawcob" and his companions may serve to while away a leisure hour for the casual reader, is the wish of the author.

CHARLES FOLLEN ADAMS.

Boston, November, 1877.

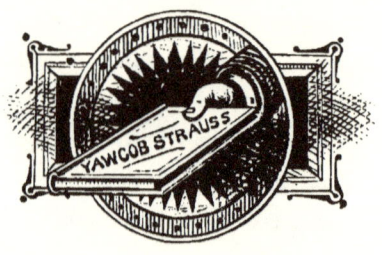

8

CONTENTS.

CONTENTS.

"I somedimes dink I schall go vild
Mit sooch a grazy poy." — Page 15.

YAWCOB STRAUSS.

I HAF von funny leedle poy,
　　Vot gomes schust to mine knee;
Der queerest schap, der createst rogue,
　　As efer you dit see.
He runs, und schumps, und schmashes dings
　　In all barts off der house:
But vot off dot? he vas mine son,
　　Mine leedle Yawcob Strauss.

11

He get der measles und der mumbs,
  Und eferyding dot's oudt;
He sbills mine glass off lager bier,
  Poots schnuff indo mine kraut.

He fills mine pipe mit Limburg cheese, —
  Dot vas der roughest chouse:
I'd dake dot vrom no oder poy
  But leedle Yawcob Strauss.

He dakes der milk-ban for a dhrum,
   Und cuts mine cane in dwo,
To make der schticks to beat it mit,—
   Mine cracious, dot vas drue!

I dinks mine hed vas schplit abart,
   He kicks oup sooch a touse:
But nefer mind; der poys vas few
   Like dot young Yawcob Strauss.

13

He asks me questions sooch as dese:
  Who baints mine nose so red?
Who vas it cuts dot schmoodth blace oudt
  Vrom der hair ubon mine hed?

Und vhere der plaze goes vrom der lamp
  Vene'er der glim I douse.
How gan I all dose dings eggsblain
  To dot schmall Yawcob Strauss?

14

I somedimes dink I schall go vild
  Mit sooch a grazy poy,
Und vish vonce more I gould haf rest,
  Und beaceful dimes enshoy;

But ven he vas ashleep in ped,
  So guiet as a ·mouse,
I prays der Lord, "Dake· anyding,
  But leaf dot Yawcob Strauss."

15

A HIGHLY-COLORED. ROMANCE.

Ben Green was a New-Hampshire boy,
　Who stood full six feet two:
A jovial chap this same Ben Green,
　Though he had oft been blue.

He loved a girl named Olive Brown,
　Who lived near Bixby's pond,
And who, despite her brunette name,
　Was a decided blonde.

16

" A highly-colored romance."

A pink of rare perfection she,
   The belle of all the town;
Though Ben oft wished her Olive Green,
   Instead of Olive Brown.

And she loved Ben, and said that nought
   Should mar their joy serene;
And, when she changed from Olive Brown,
   'Twould surely be to Green.

She kept her word in-violet,
   And vowed, ere she was wed,
Although when Brown she had Be(e)n Green,
   When Green she'd be well read.

But, ah! her young affections changed
   To Gray, a Southern fellow;
And Green turned white the news to hear,
   Though first it made him yell, oh!

19

Says he, " How can you lilac this,
    When you vowed to be true?
I'll take your fine young lover, Gray,
    And beat him till he's blue."

Then Olive Brown to crimson turned,
    And said, " Do as you say:
The country long has wished to see
    ' The Blue combined with Gray.' "

Ben Green to purple turned with rage,
    And black his brow as night;
While on the cheek of Olive Brown
    The crimson changed to white.

" O cruel Olive Brown! " says Ben,
    " I've been dun-brown by you:
Let this ' Grayback' his steps retrace,
    And take Greenback, — oh, do! "

Poor Olive Brown, what could she say,
  To sea-Green look so sad?
And so she rose, and said to him,
  " I'll go and ask my dad."

.   .   .   .

The years rolled by: Ben's raven locks
  For silver did not lack;
And Olive, with her hair of gold,
  Was glad she took Greenback.

TO BARY JADE.

THE bood is beabig brighdly, love;
  The sdars are shidig too;
While I ab gazig dreabily,
  Add thigkig, love, of you.
You caddot, oh! you caddot kdow,
  By darlig, how I biss you —
(Oh, whadt a fearful cold I've got! —
  Ck-*tish*-u! Ck-ck-*tish*-u!)

I'b sittig id the arbor, love,
  Where you sat by by side,
Whed od that calb, autubdal dight
  You said you'd be by bride.

"Ho-*rash*-o!—there it is agaid,—
Ck-*thrash*-ub! Ck-ck-*tish*-u!"—Page 26.

Oh! for wud bobedt to caress
   Add tederly to kiss you;
Budt do! we're beddy biles apart —
   (Ho-*rash*-o! Ck-ck-*tish*-u!)

This charbig evedig brigs to bide
   The tibe whed first we bet:
It seebs budt odly yesterday;
   I thigk I see you yet.
Oh! tell me, ab I sdill your owd?
   By hopes — oh, do dot dash theb!
(Codfoud by cold, 'tis gettig worse —
   Ck-*tish*-u! Ck-ck-*thrash*-eb!)

Good-by, by darlig Bary Jade!
   The bid-dight hour is dear;
Add it is hardly wise, by love,
   For be to ligger here.

25

The heavy dews are fallig fast:
A fod good-dight I wish you.
(IIo-*rash*-o! — there it is agaid —
Ck-*thrash*-ub! Ck-ck-*tish*-u!)

THE PUZZLED DUTCHMAN.

I'M a proken-hearted Deutscher,
  Vot's villed mit crief und shame.
I dells you vot der drouple ish:
  I doosn't know my name.

27

You dinks dis fery vunny, eh?
  Ven you der schtory hear,
You vill not vonder den so mooch,
  It vas so schtrange und queer.

Mine moder had dwo leedle twins;
  Dey vas me und mine broder:
Ve lookt so fery mooch alike,
  No von knew vich vrom toder.

Von off der poys vas " Yawcob,"
  Und " Hans " der oder's name:
But den it made no tifferent;
  Ve both got called der same.

Vell! von off us got tead, —
  Yaw, Mynheer, dot ish so!
But vedder Hans or Yawcob,
  Mine moder she don'd know.

28

Und so I am in drouples:
I gan't kit droo mine hed
Vedder I'm Hans vot's lifing,
Or Yawcob vot is tead!

L-E-G ON A MULE.

Did you hear of the accident, just t'other day,
That occurred to a youth of the Y. M. C. A.?

One morning, while walking out with his friend
     Neff, —
M. W. G. M. of the I. O. O. F., —

His friend exclaimed suddenly, "Look there, I
    say!
There's a chance for the S. F. P. O. C. T. A.!"

A "broth of a boy," who was just from a spree,
Was cruelly beating his m-u-l-e.

Our hero stepped up to expostulate, when
The mule kicked his a-b-d-o-m-e-n.

This doubled him up with a half-muttered phrase,
As foot No. 2 knocked him e-n-d-ways.

They bore him home gently, as gently could be,
And gave him a pint of hot l-oo-t.

A voltaic plaster they placed, *sans* delay,
Where that treacherous mule left his m-a-r-k.

31

A hip dislocated; a general jar;
Striking proofs of " one-mule p-o-w-e-r."

When the patient first spoke, what d'ye s'pose he
    did say, —
This model young man of the Y. M. C. A.?

Says he, " I'll be b-l-o-w-e-d
If ever I'll plead for a m-u-l-e!"

ECONOMY.

"THERE's nothing like economy,"
  I heard a chap remark,
Who, judging by his *tout ensemble*,
  Had issued from the ark.

He was a most peculiar man,
  With visage wan and thin,
And liquid drops of amber hue
  A-trickling down his chin.

" They tell us it's extravagant,"
  He added with a shrug,
As he deposited a quid
  Within his spacious " mug," —

" They tell us it's extravagant,
  This ' chewing of the weed ; '
But only use ' economy,'
  You'll never be in need.

" And this is how to practise it :
  Chew your tobacco well,
Using a little. at a time, —
  It nat'rally will swell ;

34

"Then take the quid and dry it, sir!" —
  'Twas thus the fellow spoke, —
" And, when you want a quiet whiff,
  Put in your pipe, and smoke.

" And, stranger, after doing this,
  If you are fond of snuff,
The ashes that are left behind
  Will serve you well enough.

" And thus," said this peculiar man
  (I fear he did but joke,)
" If you will follow my advice,   ,
  It will not end in *smoke*."

PAT'S CRITICISM.

THERE's a story that's old,
But good if twice told,
Of a doctor of limited skill,
Who cured beast and man
On the " cold-water plan,"
Without the small help of a pill.

On his portal of pine
Hung an elegant sign,
Depicting a beautiful rill,

36

" Pat, how is that for a sign ? " — PAGE 39.

And a lake where a sprite,
With apparent delight,
Was sporting in sweet dishabille.

Pat McCarty one day,
As he sauntered that way,
Stood and gazed at that portal of pine;
When the doctor with pride
Stepped up to his side,
Saying, " Pat, how is that for a sign ? "

" There's wan thing," says Pat,
" Ye've lift out o' that,
Which, be jabers! is quoite a mistake:
It's trim, and it's nate;
But, to make it complate,
Ye shud have a foine burd on the lake."

39

" Ah ! indeed ! pray, then, tell,
To make it look well,
What bird do you think it may lack ? "
Says Pat, " Of the same
I've forgotten the name,
But the song that he sings is ' Quack ! quack ! ' "

RAVENOUS BILL.

Oh! a terrible glutton was "Ravenous Bill,"
Mate of the good ship "Whippoorwill;"
And seldom it was he could get his fill;
    A fact he oft would mention.

And many a time, when eating his beef,
Would the captain tell him to "take a reef;"
But to such requests he ever was "deaf,"
    This being a bone of contention.

He cheated the sailors out of their prog,
Nor left e'en a scrap for the captain's dog:
He was such a gourmand and terrible " hog,"
    That he'd " eat you out of your house."

He thought no more of a leg of ham,
A peck of potatoes, and shoulder of lamb,
With all the " fixin's," — wine, jellies, and jam, —
    Than a cat would think of a mouse.

42

At length, on distant Southern sands
The vessel was stranded; and all the hands
Were captured by some of the savage bands
Who lived on that foreign coast.

Poor Bill was taken among the rest,
And became at once a cannibal's guest;
(No pleasant position, it must be confessed,
To wake up some morning already " dressed "
For a native's " fancy roast.")

43

For want of rations Bill had grown thin, —
Nothing, in fact, but bones and skin;
And his heathen master (as ugly as sin,
To find he'd so badly been " taken in ")
    Devised a horrible plan.

To wit: a bamboo cage he'd make,
And put in Bill, with a monstrous snake
Called the anaconda, that could easily " take "
    Most any " reasonable " man.

44

At last 'twas finished, — the cage was done ;
The snake was captured, — a monstrous one :
The natives assembled to see the " fun,"
And " *settle their Bill*," they said, as a pun,
  Referring to the " collation."

Our hero was thrust into the cage
Where the snake was coiling itself with rage,
Eager and waiting its prey to engage, —
  An *engaging* occupation.

45

As Bill and the snake met face to face,
He was folded at once in its close embrace;
And the natives, thinking he'd " ran his race,"
Began on his fate to ponder;

When — what d'ye suppose first met their eyes?
As the dust from the scene did slowly rise,
They found that Bill, to their great surprise,
Had — SWALLOWED THE ANACONDA !

SHONNY SCHWARTZ.

Haf you seen mine leedle Shonny, —
    Shonny Schwartz, —
Mit his hair so soft und yellow,
Und his face so blump und mellow;
Sooch a funny leedle fellow, —
    Shonny Schwartz?

Efry mornings dot young Shonny —
    Shonny Schwartz —
Rises mit der preak off day,
Und does his chores oup righdt avay;
For he gan vork so vell as blay, —
    Shonny Schwartz.

47

Mine Katrina says to Shonny,
     " Shonny Schwartz,
Helb your barents all you gan,
For dis life vas bud a shban:
Py und py you'll been a man,
     Shonny Schwartz."

How I lofes to see dot Shonny —
     Shonny Schwartz —
Vhen he schgampers off to schgool,
Vhere he alvays minds der rule!
For he vas nopody's fool, —
     Shonny Schwartz.

How I vish dot leedle Shonny —
     Shonny Schwartz —
Could remain von leedle poy,

48

Alvays full off life und shoy,
Und dot Time vould not annoy
                    Shonny Schwartz!

Nefer mindt, mine leedle Shonny, —
                    Shonny Schwartz;
Efry day prings someding new:
Alvays keep der righdt in view,
Und baddle, den, your own canoe,
                    Shonny Schwartz.

Keep her in der channel, Shonny, —
                    Shonny Schwartz:
Life's voyich vill pe quickly o'er;
Und den ubon dot bedder shore
Ve'll meet again, to bart no more,
                    Shonny Schwartz.

A TALE OF A NOSE.

———•—

'Twas a hard case, that which happened in Lynn.
Haven't heard of it, eh? Well then, to begin,
There's a Jew down there whom they call " Old
    Mose,"
Who travels about, and buys old clothes.

Now Mose — which the same is short for Moses —
Had one of the biggest kind of noses:
It had a sort of an instep in it,
And he fed it with snuff about once a minute.

One day he got in a bit of a row
With a German chap who had kissed his *frau*,
And, trying to punch him *à la* Mace,
Had his nose cut off close up to his face.

He picked it up from off the ground,
And quickly back in its place 'twas bound,
Keeping the bandage upon his face
Until it had fairly healed in place.

Alas for Mose! 'Twas a sad mistake
Which he in his haste that day did make;
For, to add still more to his bitter cup,
He found he had placed it *wrong side up.*   .

" There's no great loss without some gain ; "
And Moses says, in a jocular vein,
He arranged it so for taking snuff,
As he never before could get enough.

One thing, by the way, he forgets to add,
Which makes the arrangement rather bad :
Although he can take his snuff with ease,
He has to stand on his head to sneeze!

TO A DRESSMAKER.

Oh! wherefore bid me leave thy side,
  Dear Polly? I would ask.
How can I all my feelings cloak
  When in thy smiles I basque?
Nay, " Polly-nay," I cannot go!
  Oh! do not stand aloof,
When of my warm affection
  You possess, oh, wat-er-proof!

Why will you thus my feelings gore
    By sending me away?
You know it's wrong, of corset is,
    Thus to forbid my stay.
It scams as though some fell disease
    Was gnawing at my heart,
And hem-orrhage would soon ensue
    If we, perchance, should part.

Then waist the precious time no more,
    But let the parson tie us
Sew firmly that the marriage-knot
    Shall never be cut bias.
In peaceful quietude we'll float
    On life's unruffled tide,
Nor let the bustle of the world
" Pull-back " as on we glide.

YANKEE SHREWDNESS.

In a little country village,
   Not many years ago,
There lived a real " live Yankee,"
   Whom they called " Old Uncle Snow."

In trade he had no equal;
   And storekeepers would say,
" We're always ' out of pocket'
   When Snow comes round this way."

55

'Twas the custom of the villagers —
  Few of them being rich —
To trade their surplus " garden-sass "
  For groceries and " sich."

One store supplied the village
  With goods of every kind,
Including wines and liquors
  For those that way inclined.

A counter in the " sample-room "
  Was fixed up very neat;
And after every " barter-trade "
  The storekeeper would " treat."

Old Snow brought in, one morning,
  An egg fresh from the barn,
And said, " Give me a needle:
  My woman wants to darn."

"Give me another needle, 'Squire;
This egg's the same as two!" — PAGE 60.

The trade was made: the storekeeper
    Asked him to take a drink.
" I'll humor him," he said, aside,
    As the lookers-on did wink.

" Don't care, naow, ef I do," says Snow ;
    " And, as your goin' to treat,
Just put a leetle sugar in, —
    I like my liquor sweet.

" And, say, while you're about it, —
    Though I don't like to beg, —
'Twill taste a *leetle* better
    If you drop in an egg."

" All right, friend," says the grocer,
    Now being fairly " caught,"
And dropped into the tumbler
    The egg that Snow had brought !

The egg contained a double yolk.
　Says Snow, "Here, this won't do:
Give me another needle, 'Squire;
　This egg's the same as two!"

LOGIC.

'Tıs strange, but true, that a common cat
Has got *ten tails*, — just think of that!

Don't see it, eh? The fact is plain:
To prove it so I rise t'explain.

We say a cat has but one tail:
Behold how logic lifts the veil!

No cat has nine tails: don't you see
One cat has one tail more than she?

61

LOGIC.

Now add the one tail to the nine,
You'll find a full ten-tailed feline.

.   .   .   .

As Holmes has said, in his " One-Horse Shay,"
Logic is logic; that's all I say.

DER DRUMMER.

Who puts oup at der pest hotel,
Und dakes his oysders on der schell,
Und mit der frauleins cuts a schwell?
    Der drummer.

63

Who vas it gomes indo mine schtore,
Drows down his pundles on der vloor,
Und nefer schtops to shut der door?
    Der drummer.

Who dakes me py der handt, und say,
" Hans Pfeiffer, how you vas to-day?"
Und goes for peesness righdt avay?
    Der drummer.

Who shpreads his zamples in a trice,
Und dells me, " Look, und see how nice " ?
Und says I gets " der bottom price " ?
    Der drummer.

Who dells how sheap der goots vas bought,
Mooch less as vot I gould imbort,
But lets dem go as he vas " short " ?
    Der drummer.

Who says der tings vas eggstra vine, —
" Vrom Sharmany, ubon der Rhine," —
Und sheats me den dimes oudt off nine?
    Der drummer.

Who varrants all der goots to suit
Der gustomers ubon his *route*,
Und ven dey gomes dey vas no goot?
    Der drummer.

Who gomes aroundt ven I been oudt,
Drinks oup mine bier, and eats mine kraut,
Und kiss Katrina in der mout'?
　　Der drummer.

Who, ven he gomes again dis vay,
Vill hear vot Pfeiffer has to say,
Und mit a plack eye goes avay?
　　Der drummer.

C7

REPARTEE.

— •◦• —

One Mr. B——,
A joker he,
While in a jovial mood,
Tried to explain
To neighbor N——
A joke which he thought good.

His hearer, Neff,
Was very deaf,
And couldn't catch the joke;
Whereat B—— smiled,
Though slightly "riled,"
And thus to him he spoke:—

"'Tis plain to *me*
As A B C,
My dear friend, Mr. Neff!"
"Oh, yes! but then,"
. Says Mr. N——,
"You know *I'm D E F!*"

FRITZ UND I.

Mynheer, blease helb a boor oldt man
Vot gomes vrom Sharmany,
Mit Fritz, mine tog, und only freund,
To geep me gompany.

I haf no geld to puy mine pread,
   No blace to lay me down;
For ve vas vanderers, Fritz und I,
   Und sdrangers in der town.

Some beoples gife us dings to eadt,
   Und some dey kicks us oudt,
Und say, "You don'd got peesnis here
   To sdroll der schtreets aboudt!"

Vot's dot you say? — you puy mine tog
   To gife me pread to eadt!
I vas so boor as nefer vas,
   But I vas no "tead peat."

Vot, sell mine tog, mine leedle tog,
   Dot vollows me aboudt,
Und vags his dail like anydings
   Vene'er I dakes him oudt?

71

Schust look at him, und see him schump!
　　He likes me pooty vell;
Und dere vas somedings 'bout dot tog,
　　Mynheer, I vouldn't sell.

" Der collar ? "　Nein: 'tvas someding else
　　Vrom vich I gould not bart;
Und, if dot ding vas dook avay,
　　I dink it prakes mine heart.

" Vot vas it, den, aboudt dot tog,"
　　You ashk, " dot's not vor sale ? "
I dells you vot it ish, mine freund:
　　'Tish der vag off dot tog's dail ! "

"Schust look at him, und see him schump!
He likes me pooty vell." — PAGE 72.

INTEMPERANCE.

Of all the vices in our land
  Which we have reason most to dread,
Intemperance, the country's curse,
  In bold relief stands at the head.

In every sphere its steps we trace, —
  In lowly cot and mansion tall:
Alike on young and old it preys,
  Bringing its share of woe to all.

Men who could face the fiercest foe
  Unmoved, midst battles' loudest roar,
Cannot the wine-cup's charm resist,
  Nor boldly pass the dram-shop's door.

A mother's and a father's love
 Cannot the drunkard's course control:
His every wish, his every thought,
 Is centred in the flowing bowl.

Even the gentle, loving wife,
 To whom he vowed eternal love,
And children, with their tearful prayers,
 Fail his besotted heart to move.

Men of Columbia, are you slaves,
 A galling yoke like this to wear?
King Alcohol hurl from his throne,
 And place a wiser monarch there.

Then shall your loved ones' prayers be heard,
 A country's blessing be your prize;
While He who sits enthroned above
 Shall smile on you from out the skies.

LITTLE TIM'S REVENGE.

"LITTLE TIM" was the name of him
    Of whom I have to tell;
And he abode on the Western road,
    In the busy town of L——.

77

As trains went down through the little town,
  He peddled through the cars
His stock in trade, — iced lemonade,
  Cake, peanuts, and cigars.

Conductor Dunn was the only one
  Who'd not this trade allow;
And so 'twixt him and little Tim
  There always was a row.

At last one day they had a fray;
  And Timothy declared
He'd " fix old Dunn, ' as sure's a gun,' "
  If both their lives were spared.

So off he went with this intent,
  And sold his stock in trade:
His earnings hard he spent for lard,
  And started for " the grade."

(This place, you know, is where trains go
   Upon the steep hillside,
And where — with lard — it isn't hard
   To get up quite a slide.)

He took a stick, and spread it thick,
   Remarking with a smile,
" There'll be some fun when Mr. Dunn
   Commences to ' strike ile ' ! "

He lay in wait: the train was late,
　And came a-puffing hard,
With heavy load, right up the road
　To where he'd spread the lard.

They tried in vain: that fated train
　Could not ascend the grade:
The wheels would spin with horrid din;
　Yet no advance was made.

Then little Tim — 'twas bold in him —
　Cried out in accents shrill,
" Remember *me*, Conductor D.,
　When you get up the hill!"

MORAL.

Success in trade is up a grade
　That we should all ascend,
And with a will help up the hill
　Our fellow-man and friend.

When " on the road," don't incommode
  The seeker after pelf,
Or ten to one, like Mr. Dunn,
  You'll not get up yourself.

DOT BABY OFF MINE.

Mine cracious! mine cracious! shust look here
    und see
A Deutscher so habby as habby can pe!
Der beoples all dink dot no prains I haf got;
Vas grazy mit trinking, or someding like dot:
Id vasn't pecause I trinks lager und vine;
Id vas all on aggount off dot baby off mine.

Dot schmall leedle vellow I dells you vas qveer;

Not mooch pigger roundt as a goot glass off
peer;

Mit a bare-footed hed, und nose but a schpeck;

A mout dot goes most to der pack off his neck;

Und his leedle pink toes mit der rest all
combine

To gif sooch a charm to dot baby off mine.

83

I dells you dot baby vas von off der poys,
Und beats leedle Yawcob for making a noise.
He shust has pecun to shbeak goot English
    too ;
Says "Mamma" und "Papa," und somedimes
    "Ah, goo !"
You don'd find a baby den dimes oudt off nine
Dot vas qvite so schmart as dot baby off mine.

He grawls der vloor ofer, und drows dings
    aboudt,
Und poots eferyding he can find in his mout;
He dumbles der shtairs down, und falls vrom
    his chair,
Und gifes mine Katrina von derrible sckare.
Mine hair shtands like shquills on a mat borcubine
Ven I dinks off dose pranks off dot baby off mine.

Dere vas someding, you pet, I don'd likes pooty vell,
To hear in der nighdt dimes dot young Deutscher
  yell,
Und dravel der ped-room midout many clo'es,
Vhile der chills down der shpine off mine pack
  quickly goes:
Does leedle shimnasdic dricks vasn't so fine
Dot I cuts oup at nighdt mit dot baby off mine.

Vell, dese leedle schafers vas going to pe men,
Und all off dese droubles vill peen ofer den:
Dey vill vear a vhite shirt-vront inshtead off a bib,
Und vouldn't got tucked oup at nighdt in deir crib.
Vell, vell, ven I'm feeble, und in life's decline,
May mine oldt age pe cheered py dot baby off
    mine!

JOHN BARLEY-CORN, MY FOE.

John Barley-Corn, my foe, John,
 The song I have to sing
Is not in praise of you, John,
 E'en though you are a king.

JOHN BARLEY-CORN, MY FOE.

Your subjects they are legion, John,
 I find where'er I go :
They wear your yoke upon their necks,
 John Barley-Corn, my foe.

John Barley-Corn, my foe, John,
 By your despotic sway
The people of our country, John,
 Are suffering to-day.
You lay the lash upon their backs ;
 Yet willingly they go
And pay allegiance at the polls,
 John Barley-Corn, my foe.

John Barley-Corn, my foe, John,
 You've broken many a heart,
And caused the bitter tear, John,
 From many an eye to start,

The widow and the fatherless
  From pleasant homes to go,
And lead a life of sin and shame,
  John Barley-Corn, my foe.

John Barley-Corn, my foe, John,
  May Heaven speed the hour,
When Temperance shall wear the crown
  And Rum shall lose its power;
When from the East unto the West
  The people all shall know
Their greatest curse has been removed,
  John Barley-Corn, my foe!

HANS AND FRITZ.

Hans and Fritz were two Deutschers who lived
  side by side,
Remote from the world, its deceit and its pride:
With their pretzels and beer the spare moments
  were spent,
And the fruits of their labor were peace and
  content.

Hans purchased a horse of a neighbor one day,
And, lacking a part of the *Geld*, — as they say, —

Made a call upon Fritz to solicit a loan
To help him to pay for his beautiful roan.

Fritz kindly consented the money to lend,
And gave the required amount to his friend;
Remarking,—his own simple language to quote,—
" Berhaps it vas bedder ve make us a note."

The note was drawn up in their primitive way,—
" I, Hans, gets from Fritz feefty tollars to-day;"
When the question arose, the note being made,
" Vich von holds dot baper until it vas baid?"

" You geeps dot," says Fritz, " und den you vill
    know
You owes me dot money." Says Hans, " Dot ish so:
Dot makes me remempers I haf dot to bay,
Und I prings you der note und der money some
    day."

"When the question arose, the note being made,
'Vich von holds dot baper until it vas baid.'" — PAGE 92.

A month had expired, when Hans, as agreed,
Paid back the amount, and from debt he was
    freed.
Says Fritz, "Now dot settles us." Hans replies,
    "Yaw:
Now who dakes dot baper accordings by law?"

"I geeps dot now, aind't it?" says Fritz; "den,
    you see,
I alvays remempers you baid dot to me."
Says Hans, "Dot ish so: it vas now shust so blain,
Dot I knows vot to do ven I porrows again."

SEQUEL TO THE "ONE-HORSE SHAY."

Doubtless my readers all have heard
    Of the "wonderful one-horse shay"
That "went to pieces all at once"
    On the terrible earthquake-day.

96

But did they ever think of the horse,
   Or mourn the loss of him, —
The " ewe-necked bay " (who drew the " shay "),
   So full of life and vim?

He was a wonderful nag, I'm told,
   In spite of his old " rat-tail ; "
And, though he always minded the *rein*,
   He laughed at the snow and hail.

He had the finest stable in town,
   With plenty of oats and hay ;
And to the parson's oft " Hud-dup "
   He never would answer *neigh*.

To the parson's shay he was ever true,
   Though her other *felloes* were *tired :*
To live and die with his *fiancée*
   Was all that his heart desired.

He was much *attached* to his ancient mate;
  So the parson "hitched them together;"
And, when they went on their *bridle* tour,
  His heart was light as a feather.

We all remember her awful fate,
  On that sad November day,
When nothing remained but a heap of trash,
  That once was a beautiful shay.

Oh! what could *stir-up* the equine breast
  Like this fearful, harrowing blow,
Which put a *check* on his happiness,
  And filled his heart with *w(h)oa.*

As he *wheeled* about, a *shaft* of pain
  Entered his faithful breast,
As he there beheld the sad remains
  Of her whom he loved the best.

With a sudden bound and fearful snort,
  He sped away like the wind;
And a fact most queer I'll mention here, —
  No *traces* were left behind.

WOMAN.

—·•·—

WHAT is it makes a woman?
 A wealth of wavy hair,
A brow of Parian whiteness,
 And eyes like diamonds rare?

Is it cheeks that shame the roses,
 And lips like cherries, red,
With teeth of pearly beauty,
 As the poet oft hath said?

A tall and queenly creature,
 With a small and taper waist,
A Juno or a Hebe,
 Who would a throne have graced?

WOMAN.

My beau-ideal of woman
  Is a different being far;
And, if my views you wish to hear,
  I'll tell you what they are.

A heart that's warm and tender,
  A pure and holy mind;
A gentle, modest, loving one,
  Who is to others kind.

The eye may lose its lustre,
  The cheek its rosy glow,
The wavy hair no more be seen
  O'er forehead white as snow.

But the pure and gentle spirit
  Will e'er be fresh and bright:
'Tis this that makes the woman.
  Kind reader, am I right?

ZWEI LAGER.

DER night vas dark as anyding,
Ven at mine door two vellers ring,
Und say, ven I ask who vas dhere,
"Git oup und git"—und den dey schvear—
"Zwei lager."

I says, " 'Tis late : schust leaf mine house,
Und don'd pe making sooch a towse ! "
Dey only lauft me in der face,
Und say, " Pring oudt, ' Old Schweizerkase,'
    Zwei lager."

I dold dem dot der bier vas oudt ;
But dose two shaps set oup a shout,
Und said no matter if 'tvas late,
Dot dey moost haf " put on der schlate "
    Zwei lager.

" Oh ! go avay, dot is goot poys,"
Mine moder says, " und schtop der noise : "
But sdill dem vellers yellt avay ;
Und dis vas all dot dey vould say, —
    " Zwei lager."

"Vot makes you gome?" mine taughter said,
"Ven beoples all vas in deir ped:
Schust gome to-morrow ven you're dhry."
But dem two plackguards sdill did cry,
                    "Zwei lager."

"Vot means you by sooch dings as dese?
I go und 'calls for der boleese,"
Says Schneigelfritz, who lifs next door:
Dey only yellt more as pefore,
                    "Zwei lager."

"You schust holdt on a leedle vhile,"
Says mine Katrina mit a schmile:
"I vix dose shaps, you pet my life,
So dey don'd ask off Pfeiffer's vife
                    Zwei lager."

Den righdt avay she got a peese
Of goot und schtrong old Limburg cheese,
Und put it schust outside der door;
Und den ve didn't hear no more
             " Zwei lager."

A TOUGH CUSTOMER.

'Tɪs a story of a toper:
   I knew him passing well,—
A shoemaker in Natick,
   Which is oftentimes called — well —
Of course you've heard the story;
   So I will not stop to tell.

He was the hardest drinker
  For many miles around;
Though, as a waggish chap remarked,
  "*Hard* drinker! I'll be bound
He drinks about as easy
  As any man I've found!"

There chanced to be a "sample-room"
  Close by his little shop,
In which, "just to be neighborly,"
  He frequently would drop,
And "take a little something warm,"
  From gin to *gin*-ger pop.

One day he went as usual;
  And, finding no one in,
He spied upon the counter
  What he supposed was gin,
And straightway took a "nipper"
  From the bottle it was in.

Surveying, *à la connoisseur,*
 The name the bottle bore,
He found 'twas *aquafortis,*
 Which he had taken "raw," —
"A brand," quoth he, "I ne'er did see,
 And never drank before."

Just then his neighbor happened in;
 And, tremulous with fear,
(The bottle told the story,)
 He asked if he felt queer,
And if he'd have a doctor called,
 As one was living near.

"Don't worry," said the shoemaker:
 "I'm all right, I believe.
There's but one thing that's curious:
 I really can't conceive
Why, when I wipe my mouth, it burns
 A hole right through my sleeve!"

DOT POODLE DOG.

Mine cracious, vot a gountry,
   Und vot a beoples too!
I feel so bad, already,
   I don'd know vot to do.

I had von leedle poodle dog,
   So handsome vot couldt been;
Und alvays, vheresoe'er I vent,
   Dot poodle dog vas seen.

DOT POODLE DOG.

He youst to vollow me aroundt,
 In schpite off rain und hail;
Und, oh, der comfort vot I dook
 In der vag off dot dog's tail!

Von day I missed mine Schneider,
 (Dot vas der poodle's name;)
Und, though I vistled all aroundt,
 Dot poodle didn't came.

I looked about der sausage-shops,
 (Vhere dey cut some vunny capers,)
Und dold dot he vas schtrayed or stoldt
 In all der daily bapers.

I hunted eferyvhere aroundt,—
 Oup hill, und down der dale;
Und all der beoples lauft at me
 To hear dot poodle's tale.

"He used him vashing vindows off:
Mine cracious, dot vas qveer!" — PAGE 113.

Von morning early I vas oudt,
   A valking oup der schtreet,
Ven righdt avay I seen a sight
   Vot schtopped mine heart to beat.

Mine cracious! vot you dink it vas
   Dot villed me mit surbrise?
'Tvas leedle Schneider vot vas losht,
   Righdt dhere pefore mine eyes!

You know schust how id is myself
   Ven somedings stardt you, — aindt id?
Vell, ven I saw dot poodle dog,
   Py shings! I almost vainted!

A darky had him on a pole,
   Mit pails off vater near.
He used him *vashing vindows off:*
   Mine cracious, dot vas qveer!

He dipped him righdt indo der pail,
Schust like he vas a rag:
Der life vas oudt off dot poodle dog;
Der tail had losht its vag!

MISPLACED SYMPATHY.

Little Benny sat one evening,
  Looking o'er his picture-book:
Suddenly his mother noticed
  On his face a troubled look.

He was gazing on a picture, —
  "Christians in the early days,"
When the cruel tyrant Nero
  Harassed them in various ways.

'Twas a family of Christians,
  Torn by lions fierce and wild,
In the horrible arena,
  Which had thus distressed the child.

Thinking it a golden moment
   To impress his youthful mind
With our freedom, dearly purchased,
   And by martyrs' blood refined,

His good mother told the story
   Of their persecutions sore,
While he listened, all attention,
   And the picture pondered o'er.

" See, my child, those hungry lions,
   How upon the group they fall!
'Tis a sight, my precious darling,
   That the bravest might appall."

Then, with little lip a-quiver,
   " Mamma, look!" says little Benny:
" Little lion in the corner,
   Mamma, *isn't gettin' any!*"

" Little lion in the corner,
    Mamma, isn't gettin' any!" — PAGE 116.

VOT I LIKE UND DON'D LIKE.

I DON'D dink mooch off dose fine shaps
    Vot lofe aboudt der schtreet,
Und nefer pays der landlady
    For vot dey haf to eat;

Who gifes der tailor notings,
  Und makes der laundress vait,
Und haf deir trinks off lager bier
  All "put ubon der schlate."

I don'd dink mooch off vimmin, too,
  Who dink it vas deir "schpeer"
To keep oup vine abbearances,
  Und lif in "Grundy's" fear;
Who dress demselves mit vine array
  To flirt ubon der schtreet,
Und leaf deir moders at der tub
  To earn der bread dey eat.

I don'd like men dot feel so pig
  Ven dey haf plenty *geld*,
Who vas as Lucifer so broud,
  Und mit conceit vas schvelled.

Who dinks more off deir horse und dog
  As off a man dot's poor,
Und lets der schtarving und der sick
  Go hungry vrom der door.

I don'd dink mooch off dem dot holdt
  So tight ubon a tollar,
Dot, if 'tvas only shust alife,
  'Tvould make it shcream und holler.
Vy don'd dey keep it on der move,   '
  Not hide avay und lock it?
Dey gannot take it ven dey die:
  Der shroud don'd haf a pocket!

.   .   .   .

I like to see a hand dot's brown,
  Und not avraid off vork;
Dot gifes to dose vot air in need,
  Und nefer tries to schirk:

121

VOT I LIKE UND DON'D LIKE.

A man dot meets you mit a schmile,
  Und dakes you py der hand,
Shust like dey do vhere I vas born,
  In mine own vaterland, —

Vhere bier-saloons don'd keep a schlate;
  Vhere tailors get deir pay,
Und vashervimmin get der schtamps
  For vork dey dake avay;
Vhere *frauleins* schtick righdt to der voik
  So schteady as a glock,
Und not go schtrutting droo der schtreets
  Shust like a durkey-cock;
Vhere blenty und brosperity
  Schmile ubon efery hand:
Dot ist der Deutscher's paradise;
  Das ist das Vaterland.

THE WIDOW MALONE'S PIG.

THE Widow Malone had a beautiful pig;
  No one had its equal from Cork to Killarney:
And Paddy McCabe had his eye on the same;
  A roguish chap he, full of mischief and blarney.

This beautiful pig fairly haunted his dreams;
  And he swore, that, unless he was sadly mistaken,
He would feast off his ribs upon St. Patrick's
    Day,
  And even the widow should not "save his
    bacon."

One morning the widow went out to the pen,
  Pail in hand, with the first streak of dawn,
When, lo! it was vacant; no piggy was there:
  The sweet little creature was gone!

Straightway to the priest for assistance she went,
  Who asked her the cause of her grief.
"Och! your riverince," says she, "'tis me pig
    that is gone!
And I think Pat McCabe is the thief."

Soon after Pat came to the priest to "confess,
  And told of his theft from the Widow Malone.
"Take it back," says the priest, "without any
    delay!"
  "Sure I've ate it, your riverince!" says Pat
    with a groan.

" The Widow Malone had a beautiful pig;
No one had its equal from Cork to Killarney." — Page 123.

"Ah, Pat!" says the priest, "at the great 'judg-
ment-day,'
When you meet the widow and pig face to face,
What excuse will you give for your terrible sin?
I'm thinking you'll go to a very bad place."

"Will the widdy and pig *both* be there?" says Pat.
"To be sure," says the priest, "to accuse you
of sin."
"Will, thin," replies Paddy, "I'll say,'*Here's your pig!*
By St. Patrick, I'll niver molist him agin!'"

127

A TRAPPER'S STORY.

" "Twas a moonlight night," the trapper began,
  As we lay by the bright camp-fire, —
" Come, fill up your pipes, and pile on the brands,
  And gather a little nigher, —

128

" 'Twas a moonlight night when Bet and I —
Bet, she's the old mare, you know —
Started for camp on our lonely route,
    O'er the dreary waste of snow.

" I had been to the ' clearing' that afternoon
    For powder and ball, and whiskey too ;
For game was plenty, furs in demand,
    And plenty of hunting and trapping to do.

" I had no fear of the danger that lurked
    In the region through which my journey lay,
Till Bet of a sudden pricked up her ears,
    And sniffed the air in a curious way.

" I knew at once what the danger was
    As Bet struck out at a 'forty gait:
'Twas life or death for the mare and me,
    And all I could do was to trust to fate.

" *Wolves on our track*, ten miles from home!
   A pleasant prospect that, — eh, boys?
I could see them skulking among the trees,
   And the woods re-echoed their hideous noise.

" At last, as their numbers began to swell,
   They bolder grew, and pressed us close:
So ' Old Pill-Driver ' I brought to bear,
   And gave the leader a leaden dose.

" Now, you must know, if you draw the blood
   On one of the sneaking, ravenous crew,
The rest will turn on the double-quick,
   And eat him up without more ado.   .

" This gave me a chance to load my gun,
   With just a moment to breathe and rest;
When on they came! a-gaining fast,
   Though Bet was doing her level best.

"So ' Old Pill-Driver ' I brought to bear,
And gave the leader a leaden dose." — PAGE 130.

" I began to think it was getting hot.
  ' Pill-Driver,' says I, ' this will never do :
Talk to 'em again ! ' You bet she did ;
  And right in his tracks lay number two.

" Well, boys, to make a long story short,
  I picked them off till but one was left ;
But he was a whopper, you'd better believe, —
  A reg'lar mammoth in size and heft.

" Yes, he was the last of the savage pack ;
  For, as they had followed the nat'ral law,
They had eaten each other as fast as they fell,
  Till all were condensed in his spacious maw."

JOHNNY JUDKINS.

JOHNNY JUDKINS was a vender
  Of a patent liquid blacking:
Johnny Judkins he was witty,
  And for " check " he was not lacking.

Johnny stood upon the corner,
  Selling polish day by day,
And would " polish off " a party
  Who had any thing to say.

Johnny's stereotyped expression
  Was, " Now, gents, at the beginnin'
I would state this magic polish
  Will not soil the finest linen."

Johnny then its other virtues
  Rapidly would mention o'er,
And would sell his gaping hearers
  From a dozen to a score.

Hans von Puffer bought a bottle,
  Which upon his shirt-front white,
As he used it without caution,
  Left a spot as black as night.

Back to Johnny went Von Puffer,
  Saying, " Vot vas dot you zay?
'Tvill not soil der vinest linen?
  See mine shirt-vrond righdt avay!

" Vot vas dot ubon mine bosom ?
　Von't you dold me, ef you blease !
Shust you gife me pack mine moncy,
　Or I goes vor der boleese ! "

Johnny looked upon the Deutscher
　With a bland and childlike smile ;
Then upon the crowd before him,
　Who enjoyed the sport meanwhile.

" Gentlemen," says Johnny Judkins,
　" As I said in the beginnin',
This 'ere patent liquid polish
　Will not soil the *finest* linen.

" As for that," says Johnny Judkins,—
　Pointing where the spot of crock
Showed upon Von Puffer's bosom
　Like a black sheep in a flock,—

"Vot vas dot ubon mine bosom?
Von't you dold me, ef you blease!" — Page 136.

" As for that," repeated Johnny,
" If you call *that* linen fine,
I would merely say, my hearers,
Your opinion is not mine."

Johnny Judkins still continues
Selling blacking by the ton.
Hans von Puffer chalks that bosom
Every time he puts it on.

THE LOST PET.

Oh, list! while I tell
Of the fate that befell
A pet that was dear unto me, —
A black-and-tan pup.
Oh! bitter the cup
Prepared by that " Heathen Chinee "
For me,
The friend of those venders of tea.

140

This young black-and-tan
Away from me ran, —
An act which I did not foresee;
And, though I did seek
For over a week
To find him, it was not to be.
You'll see,
'Twas the work of that sinful ·Chinee.

His name was Ah-Bet,
(Not the name of my pet,
But of him of Chinese pedigree;)
And he kept a small shop,
And had the best " chop "
Of tit-bits from over the sea,
That he
Obtained from his far-famed *patrie.*

141

He had " chow-chow," that tickles
The lover of pickles,
Though with me it did never agree;
And things filled with spice,
Which may have been mice, —
They looked enough like them, — dear me !
To see
Such food in the "land of the free."

One day I'd a friend
Who was coming to spend
The day, and take dinner with me:
So I went to Ah-Bet,
And told him to get
A rabbit " and fixin's ; " and he
Said "*Oui*,"
In a manner quite Frenchy to see.

142

"And brought to the light
A tag, with inscription, 'Toby.'" — PAGE 145.

The clock had struck one:
The dinner was done,
And served up with steaming Bohea.
  " 'Tis excellent fare,
  This rabbit, or hare,
Whichever it may be," said he,
    (*Mon ami:*)
" You've a prize in that Heathen Chinee."

Just then in the dish
I noticed him fish
For something he thought he could see,
  That didn't look right;
  And brought to the light
A tag, with inscription, " Toby."
    Ah me!
'Twas that of my lost *favori!*

145

THE SOLDIER'S GRAVE.

How many of our honored dead
  Now sleep beneath the Southern sod,
With nought to mark their resting-place;
  Their graves unknown, except to God!

Far from their loving ones at home
  They died, their country's flag to save, —
That flag the emblem of the free,
  That struck the shackles from the slave.

No loving mother's gentle hand
  Was there to hold the weary head;
No mourning friends assembled round
  The gallant soldier's dying bed.

The suit of blue his only shroud;
   His funeral dirge the cannon's roar:
There, where he fell, the soldier lay,
   His battles fought, his hardships o'er.

Though flowers may not his grave adorn,
   Though loving friends may not be near,
A country, which he died to save,
   Will hold his memory ever dear.

New Illustrated Books.

ABIDE WITH ME.

The favorite Sacred Song, by Rev. HENRY FRANCIS LYTE. With Full-page and Initial Illustrations, designed by Miss L. B. Humphrey, engraved by John Andrew & Son. Small 4to. Cloth, gilt . **$2 00**

NEARER, MY GOD, TO THEE.

The universal Praise Song, in Church and Home, by SARAH FLOWER ADAMS. Full-page and Initial Illustrations, designed by Miss L. B. Humphrey, engraved by John Andrew & Son. Small 4to. Cloth, gilt.. **2 00**

OH, WHY SHOULD THE SPIRIT OF MORTAL BE PROUD?

By WILLIAM KNOX. "President Lincoln's Favorite." With Full-page and Initial Illustrations, designed by Miss L. B. Humphrey, engraved by John Andrew & Son. Small 4to. Cloth, gilt........ **2 00**

BALLADS OF BRAVERY.

Edited by GEORGE M BAKER. With 40 full-page illustrations. Large 4to. Elegantly bound in Red, Black, and Gold. New style...... **3 50**

BALLADS OF HOME.

Edited by GEORGE M. BAKER. With 40 full-page illustrations. Large 4to. Elegantly bound in Red, Black, and Gold. New style...... **3 50**

BALLADS OF BEAUTY.

Edited by GEORGE M. BAKER. With 40 full-page illustrations. Large 4to. Elegantly bound in Red, Black, and Gold. New style...... **3 50**

ÆSOP'S FABLES.

A new and elegant edition with over one hundred illustrations. Large 4to, gilt. In Red, Black, and Gold.............................. **3 50**

BABY BALLADS.

By UNO. With 40 illustrations. Small 4to......................... **1 00**

LITTLE SONGS FOR LITTLE PEOPLE.

By MRS. MARY ANDERSON. A new edition, with numerous illustrations. Small 4to... **1 00**

LITTLE SONGS.

By MRS. FOLLEN. A new and elegant edition. Small 4to........... **1 00**

LITTLE PEOPLE OF GOD,

And what the Poets have said of them. Edited by MRS. GEORGE L. AUSTIN. A choice collection of the best poems on childhood. 4to. Cloth. Illustrated.. **2 00**

The Publishers offer the trade extra discount on these books for special bills.

LEE & SHEPARD, PUBLISHERS, BOSTON

ABIDE WITH ME.

By Rev. HENRY FRANCIS LYTE.

Illustrated from designs by Miss L. B. HUMPHREY.

Small 4to, Gilt, Ornamental Covers, Price, $2.

Uniform with the illustrated edition of

NEARER, MY GOD, TO THEE,

AND

OH, WHY SHOULD THE SPIRIT OF MORTAL BE PROUD?

Its author was a highly educated clergyman of the Church of England, endowed with fine poetical gifts, who, after his conversion, desiring to glorify the Father by laboring for the poor, entered upon his mission with new views, new consolations, and a new zeal, consecrating all his powers, his service, and poetic gifts to religion. Gentle and childlike in spirit, he served faithfully till his death — which was that of a happy Christian poet. Like George Herbert and Charles Wesley, he sang while his strength lasted, and then quietly waited, till, "rising from the sleep of death, he joined the hallelujahs of heaven."

This poem was written under the following peculiar circumstances, — as related in " The Story of the Hymns : " —

" It was the autumn of 1847; the gloom of winter was already settling upon the coast, and the pomps of decay tinging the leaves. The pastor, who was now preparing to leave the parish, and who seemed like one already hovering over the verge of the grave, determined to speak to his dear people once more, perhaps for the last time. He dragged his attenuated form into the pulpit, and delivered his parting discourse, while the great tears rolled down the hardy faces of the worshippers. He then administered the Lord's Supper to his spiritual children. Tired and exhausted, but with his heart still swelling with emotion, he went home. The old poetic inspiration came over him, and he wrote the words and music of his last song. He had prayed that his last breath might be spent, ' swan-like,'—

' In songs that may not die,' —

and this effort was to prove a literal answer to his prayer. The poem composed under these interesting circumstances was the well-known hymnchant beginning, —

'Abide with me: fast falls the eventide.' " .

Sold by all Booksellers, and sent by mail, postpaid, upon receipt of price.

LEE & SHEPARD - - Publishers,
BOSTON, MASS.

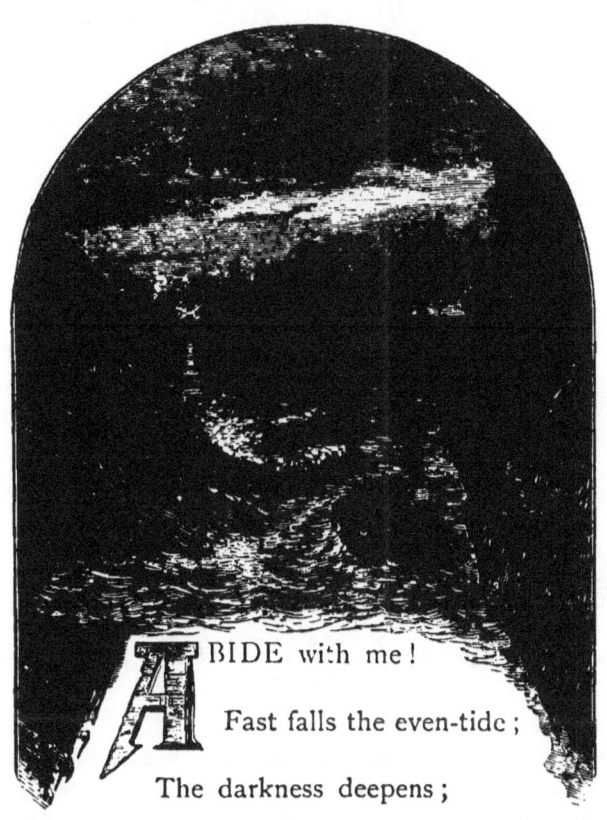

BIDE with me!

Fast falls the even-tide;

The darkness deepens;

Lord, with me abide!

"THE FOUNTAIN OF TREVI."

SPECIMEN OF ILLUSTRATIONS TO "QUINNEBASSET GIRLS."

"THEY RODE SLOWLY."

and other poems.

981177

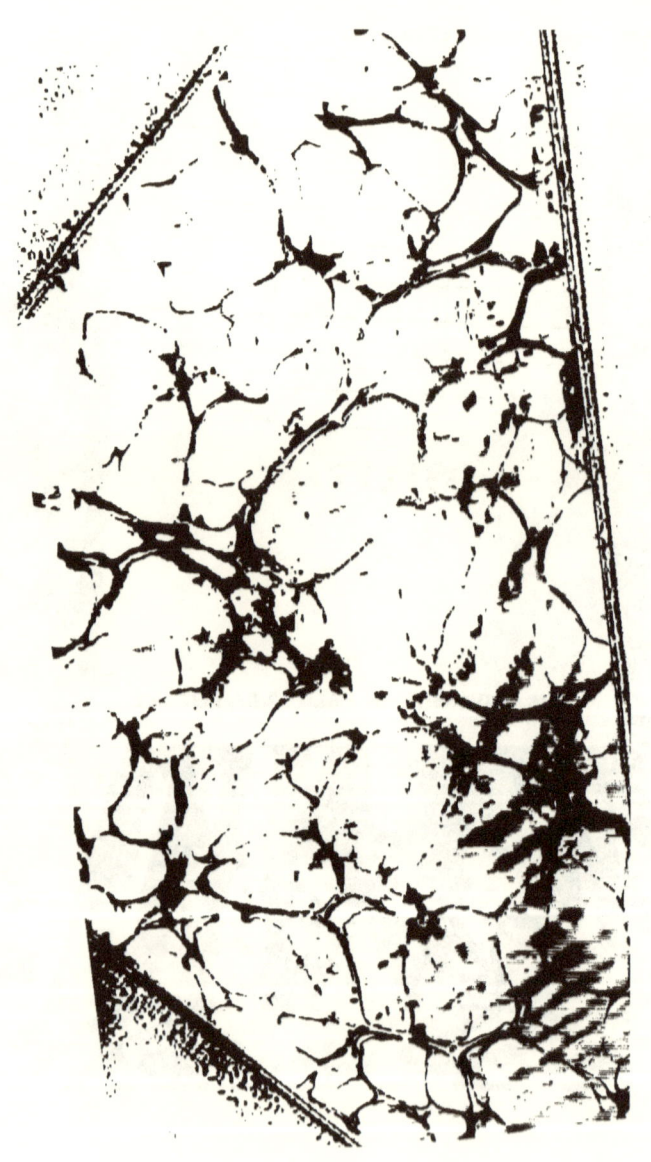